To Tommy,
    May you always ~~~~~
brave, and kind!
    ♡ Nick. Costello

Patti's PREDICAMENT

GIRLS ROCK

written by
Vicki Costello

This book is heartfully dedicated to my
Mr. Wonderful, who always believes in me.
Also, to all of my former and future Costelleans.

V.C.

Mrs. Becker teaches third grade.

She loves her students
and she loves to teach!

On Monday morning when Mrs. Becker told the class to begin their math work, Patti said, "Mrs. Becker, my tummy hurts. I can't do my math work."

When it was time to read, Patti said, "Mrs. Becker, I need to get a bandage for my finger. I can't read right now."

Then when it was time to write, Patti said,
"I have a headache. I can't write now."

Patti was really having
a bad day and had a
very sad face.

Mrs. Becker smiled
kindly and said, "Patti,
just do your best and
get your work done."

At lunch time, Mrs. Becker peeked into the cafeteria to check on Patti.

Patti was eating her sandwich and apple slices as well as chatting with her friends.

This made Mrs. Becker smile!

On Tuesday morning when Mrs. Becker told the class to begin their math work, Patti said, "Mrs. Becker, my arm hurts. I can't do my math work now."

When it was time to read, Patti said, "Mrs. Becker, I need to get some ice for my sore ankle. I can't read now."

Then when it was time to write, Patti said, "I have an earache. I can't write now."

Mrs. Becker nodded and said, "Patti, just do your best and get your work done."

During recess, Mrs. Becker put on her sunglasses and hat so she could walk around the playground.

She noticed Patti playing with several friends.

First they were playing tag.
Then they were jumping rope.

This made Mrs. Becker grin!

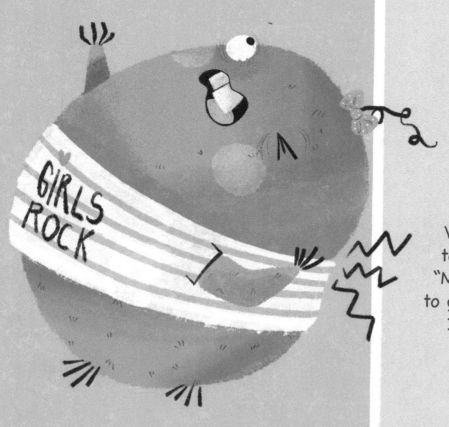

When it was time
to read, Patti said,
"Mrs. Becker, I need
to go to the bathroom.
I can't read now."

On Wednesday morning when Mrs. Becker
told the class to begin their math work,
Patti said, "Mrs. Becker, my neck hurts.
I can't do my math work."

Mrs. Becker said, "Patti, just do your best and get your work done."

Then when it was time to write, Patti said, "I have a sore tooth. I can't write now."

After school, Mrs. Becker went
to the gym to check on Patti.

Patti was at basketball practice and
she was working hard with her team.

This made Mrs. Becker beam!

On Thursday morning, Mrs. Becker told
the class to begin their math work just
as the school nurse said over the intercom,
"Mrs. Becker, can you please bring your class to
the office? It is time for their vision screening."

Mrs. Becker lined up all of her students and walked them quietly to Mr. James' office.

The students took turns covering one eye and reading the letters on his eye chart and then covering the other eye and reading more letters on his eye chart. Mr. James wrote down the smallest line of letters each student could read clearly.

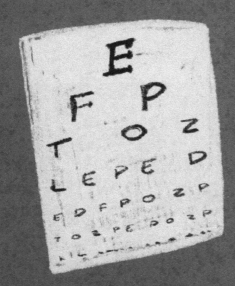

Then it was Patti's turn...

"Patti, cover your right eye with your hand and read the second line of letters."
"Um...4...G...S....E," Patti said.

Mr. James recorded her answers and said,
"Patti, cover your left eye and read the third line of letters."
"Okay...A...3...7...L."

"Hmmm, thank you Patti. You may return to your classroom," said Mr. James

Mr. James handed Patti's results to Mrs. Becker.
Mrs. Becker felt sad and frowned.

Patti returned to the classroom in time to begin math work. Mrs. Becker wrote the problems on the board in very large print.

Patti sat quietly and completed her work!

When it was time to read, Mrs. Becker read them a book.

Patti sat quietly and listened!

Then when it was time to write, Mrs. Becker told the class to raise their hands and share their favorite part of the book with the class, instead.

Patti raised her hand and shared her favorite part of the book!

Patti had a very good day and had a very happy face.

Mrs. Becker smiled and said, "Patti, can you please give this note to your parents. It is from Mr. James."

On Friday morning when Mrs. Becker asked
the class to begin their math work, Patti was not in class.

When it was time to read, Patti's desk was still empty.

When it was time to write, there was
a knock at the classroom door.

Mrs. Becker opened the door and Patti entered wearing the cutest pair of teal glasses that Mrs. Becker had ever seen!

Patti was smiling ear to ear and asked, "Mrs. Becker, is it writing time?"

Mrs. Becker smiled and said, "Patti, you are just in time!"

CPSIA information can be obtained
at www.ICGtesting.com
Printed in the USA
LVHW071909021021
699326LV00002B/2